First published in 2015
by Hodder Children's Books

Copyright © Pat Hutchins 2015

Hodder Children's Books, an imprint of Hachette Children's Group. Part of Hodder & Stoughton.
Carmelite House, 50 Victoria Embankment, London EC4Y 0DZ.

A catalogue record of this book is available from the British Library.

ISBN 978 1 444 91828 1

Printed in China

An Hachette UK Company

www.hachette.co.uk

Where, Oh Where, is Rosie's Chick?

Pat Hutchins

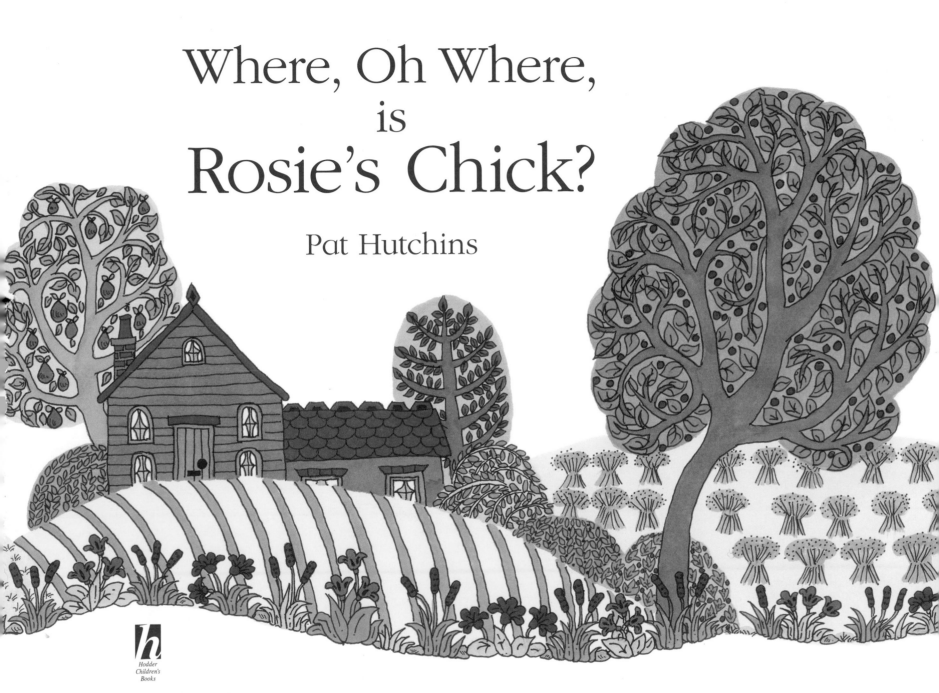

Hodder
Children's
Books

A division of Hachette Children's Group

For Susan,
who hatched Rosie,
and Anne,
who hatched Rosie's chick.

- P.H.

Hooray!
Rosie the hen
has laid
an egg.

And, at last, her egg is hatching...

But, oh no!

Where is little baby chick?

Rosie looked under the hen house,

but little baby chick wasn't there.

She looked in the basket,
but little baby chick wasn't there.

She looked behind the wheelbarrow,
but little baby chick wasn't there either.

She looked across the fields,

but she still couldn't find little baby chick!

She looked through the straw,
but little baby chick wasn't there either.

Where, oh where, is little baby chick?

BEHIND YOU!

Then Rosie and her little
baby chick went for a walk...

The end.

Praise for *Rosie's Walk*:

"A sunny, slapstick silent comedy."
NEW YORK TIMES

"The pictures tell an action-packed story full of drama and surprise."
JULIA ECCLESHERE, GUARDIAN

"The highly patterned red, orange and yellow graphics are as fresh and funny as they were in 1968 and will make 2-4s howl with laughter."
THE TIMES

"All young children will enjoy the tale of Rosie the hen and her walk around the farm followed by a hungry but thankfully hapless fox."
SUNDAY EXPRESS

"A delightful tale from a celebrated author."
NURSERY EDUCATION

"The perfect picture book for teaching children to read."
BOOKS FOR KEEPS